DARK PLACES

A SHORT STORY COLLECTION

SHERRILYN
KENYON

WITH A MADAUG HISHINUMA CONTRIBUTION

OLIVER
HEBER
BOOKS

A Day In The Life

SHERRILYN KENYON

Chapter One

"Ding dong, the bitch is dead."

Elliot Lawson looked up from her Blackberry email to laugh at her assistant Lesley Dane. "And there is much rejoicing."

Dressed in a pink sweater and floral skirt, Lesley flounced around Elliot's tiny office with a wide smile before she added yet another bulging manuscript to the top of the mountain of manuscripts in Elliot's inbox. Was it just her or did that thing grow higher by the heartbeat? It was like some bad horror movie.

The Stack That Wouldn't Die.

"Just think," Lesley continued, "no more emails with her calling us names and complaining about everything from title to synopsis to... you know, everything."

. . .

That was the upside.

The downside? "And no more selling three million copies the opening day either." While Helga East had been the biggest pain in the ass to ever write a book, her thrillers had set so many records for sales that her unexpected death left a huge hole in their publishing program. One that would take twenty or more authors to fill.

Elliot's stomach cramped at that reality and at the fact that she'd just lost her prolific star pony in the publishing race. "What are we going to do?"

"We'll build another blockbuster."

She scoffed at her assistant. "You say that like it's an easy thing to do. Trust me, if it was, every book we published would be one." And that didn't happen by a long shot. They didn't even break even on ninety percent of them.

"Yeah, but still the bitch *is* dead."

It was probably wrong to be happy about that, but like Lesley, she couldn't help feeling a little relief. Helga had been a handful.

Oh, who was she fooling? Helga had been the biggest bitch on the planet. A chronic thorn who had given Elliot two ulcers and a permanent migraine for four solid months around the release of any of Helga's books. In fact, Helga had been screaming at her over the phone when she'd had a heart attack and keeled over. It was creepy really. One second she'd been calling Elliot's intelligence and parentage into question, and in the next...

Dead.

Life was so fragile and tragedies like this rammed that home.

Lesley's phone rang. She left to answer it while Elliot stared out her tiny window at the red brick building next door where another drone like her worked a sixty hour a week job at the bank over there. She didn't know his name and yet she knew a lot about him. He brought his lunch to work, preferred a brown tweed jacket, and he tugged at his hair whenever he was frustrated. It made her wonder what unconscious habits she had that he'd pegged about her. They'd never waved to or acknowledged each other in any way, yet she could see enough personal details about him that she'd know him anywhere.

Not wanting to think about that depressing fact, she returned her attention to the cover proofs piled in front of her. One was for

Helga's next book—the one she'd been working on when Helga had died.

Her phone dinged, letting her know she had a new email.

Sighing, she picked up her Blackberry and looked at it.

For a full minute she couldn't breathe as she saw the last name she'd ever expected to see again.

Helga East.

Relax. It's just an old email that was forwarded by someone else or one that'd gotten lost in cyberspace for a couple of days.

No need to panic or be concerned in the least. It was nothing.

Still, her stomach habitually knotted as she opened it.

Tell me honestly, Elliot, does it hurt to be that stupid? Really? What part of that heinous, godawful cover did you think I'd approve of? I hate green. How many times do we have to have this argument? Get that bimbo off the cover and take that stupid font and tell Creative to stick it on the cover of someone too moronic to know better.

H.

PS the title, Nymphos Abroad, is disgusting, demeaning and insulting. Change it or I'll have another talk with your boss about how incompetent you are.

She sucked her breath in sharply as she realized the email pertained to the cover on her desk.

A cover Helga had never seen. It'd only arrived that morning.

Two days after Helga's funeral.

Yeah, there was no way it was Helga. Anger whipped through her as she hit reply to the email. "Okay, Les, stop messing with me. I'm not in the mood and this isn't funny."

A second later, a response came back.

Les? Are you on drugs? Surely you can't afford them on your pathetic salary. I've seen the cheap shoes you wear and that sorry excuse for a designer handbag that you think no one will know you bought in Times Square for five dollars. Now quit stalling, stop reading your email and call down to Art and get me a cover worthy of my status.

She looked out her door to see Lesley on the phone, her back to her computer. Definitely not her pretending to be Helga.

But someone was. And they were doing a good job of it, too.

Who is this? she typed.

Helga, you nincompoop. Who did you think

it was? Your mother? I swear, is there no one up there with a single brain cell in their head?

It couldn't be. Yet the return address in the header was Helga's. It was an email addy she knew all too well. Numberonewriter@heast.com.

Maybe one of Helga's heirs was messing with her. But why would they do such a thing? Surely they wouldn't be as cruel as Helga had been?

Then again, maybe it was genetic. Meanness like Helga's had seemed to be hardwired into her DNA. It was what the lonely old woman had lived and breathed.

Her heirs wouldn't be able to see that cover. They'd have no way of knowing what was on it.

There was that. No one outside of their publishing house had seen it.

Another email appeared. *Why are you still sitting at your desk, staring into space? I told you what to do. Get me a decent cover, you twit.*

A chill went down her spine. One so deep that she actually jumped when her cell phone went off, signaling her that she had a new voice mail message.

Weird, she hadn't heard it ring.

Reaching down, she pulled it up and accessed her box.

"I will not stand for that tawdry, disgusting cover. Do you hear me, Elliot? I want it gone, right now. Hit delete."

Her heart pounded at a voice she'd know anywhere.

Helga.

"You all right?"

She looked up at Lesley who was staring at her from the doorway. "I... I..." Pulling the phone down, she hit the four button to make it repeat. "Tell me what you hear?"

Lesley put it up to her ear. After a few seconds, she scowled. "Man, I hate those pocket dials where all you get is background noise. What kind of imbecile doesn't lock their phone?" She handed it back.

Baffled, Elliot replayed it and held it up to her ear to listen. It was still Helga, plain as the desk in front of her. "It's not a pocket dial. Can't you hear her?" She held it back out to Lesley.

Again, Lesley listened. "There's no voice, El. Just a lot of background sounds like trucks on the highway or something, and someone laughing. You okay?"

Apparently not. How could they listen to the same thing and yet hear such radically different messages?

She hung up her phone and gave Leslie a forced smile. "Fine. Stressed. Tired."

Crazy...

Clearing her throat, she put the phone on her desk. "Did you need something?"

"Just reminding you about the marketing meeting in five minutes."

"Thanks." Elliot gathered her notes for the meeting while she tried her best not to think about the phone call and emails from a writer who was dead. It wasn't Helga. Some sick psycho was messing with her head.

Or it was a friend with a sorry excuse for a sense of humor.

Yeah, that would be her luck.

It's not funny, folks. But the one thing she knew from being an editor was that humor was subjective. How many times had Helga written something that she'd rolled her eyes over, only to have the billions of readers out there find it hysterical?

Maybe I'm being Punk'd.

Could happen... If only she was lucky enough for Ashton Kutcher to pop out of a closet.

But there was no Ashton in the meeting. Only mind-numbing details about books they'd already gone over a million times that left her attention free to contemplate who was being cruel and highly unusual to her.

Maybe it's someone in this meeting.

She looked around her coworkers, most of whom appeared as stressed out and bored as she was.

No, they were too involved with their own lives to care about harassing her.

Why was this meeting taking so long?

It was hellacious.

Subversively, she glanced down at her watch and did a double take. Was it just her or was the second hand making a thirty second pause between each tick?

By the time the meeting was out, she felt like she'd been stretched on the rack. Oh good Lord, why did they have to have these all the time? What Torquemada SOB thought this was a good idea?

But at least it was finally over. She breathed a sigh in relief as she gathered her things and left.

The moment she was back in her office, she checked her email. There were ninety, n-i-n-e-t-y, messages from her wannabe Helga stalker.

She deleted them without reading.

Trying to put it out of her mind, she

turned around in her chair to look at her "friend" in the other building.

For once his office was dark. How strange. He never left early. But her attention was quickly drawn to something that was being reflected in the darkness of her glass.

Something someone had attached to her cork bulletin board that she'd hung next to her door.

With a gasp, she turned around to see if her mind was playing tricks.

It wasn't.

Her heart in her throat, she got up and went to it. As she reached for it, her hand shook.

Someone had taken Helga's cover and pinned it with a blood red tack to the board. It had nasty comments written all over it with a black magic marker. Worse? The handwriting looked just like Helga's.

Terror filled her as she ripped it down, then made her way to Lesley's desk. Lesley paused mid stroke on the keyboard to look up at her.

"Who did you let into my office while I was at the meeting?"

"No one."

"Someone went in there." She held the marked up print out toward Lesley.

She frowned. "Why are you showing me that?"

"I want you to tell me who wrote on it."

Her scowl deepened. "You did, Elliot."

What? She snatched it back and turned it over.

All of Helga's writing was gone from it. Now the only pen marks were where someone had approved the art by placing Elliot's initials in the margins. "I didn't do this."

Lesley looked at it carefully. "It's your handwriting, hon. Believe me, I know."

But Elliott hadn't written on it. Not even a little bit.

How was this possible? How?

Her head started throbbing. Without another word, she returned to her office and sat down to stare at the mechanical of the cover sans the nastiness.

"I'm losing my mind." She had to be. There was no other explanation for what was going on.

The skin on the back of her neck tingled as if someone was watching her. She turned around in her chair to inspect her office.

She was alone.

Still the feeling persisted. And even more

concerning was the prickly sensation that something wasn't right.

I'm being haunted...

Yeah, that's what it felt like. That uneasy feeling in the pit of her stomach. Something evil was in the room with her. It was all but breathing down her neck.

Panicked, she shot back to Lesley's desk. She needed to feel connected to someone alive.

Lesley gave her an arch stare. "You're pale. Is something wrong?"

If not for the fear of Lesley thinking her insane, she'd confide in her. But no one needed to know her suspicion. "Doing research for a book on my desk. You know anything about the paranormal?"

"Not really, but...."

"What?"

"I have an exorcist on my speed dial."

Elliott burst into nervous laughter. Until she realized Lesley wasn't joking. "You're serious?"

"Absolutely. My best friend in the world is an exorcist."

"Who in the world has a friend who's an exorcist?"

She held her phone up and grinned. "Me. What'cha want me to check?"

"Um... do you think I could speak with your friend?"

Her grin turned into another frown. "Sure. Her name's Trisha Yates. You want me to email it to you?"

"Please." Even though she was still skittish about her office, Elliott returned and closed her door. There was no need in Lesley overhearing this particular conversation.

Out of habit, she glanced to the office across the way.

Her heart stopped beating.

He was hanging from the ceiling, swinging in front of his desk.

No! It wasn't possible. She closed her eyes and covered them with her hands. *It's not real. It's not real...*

But it was. As soon as she opened her eyes, she saw him across the way. Medics were swarming his office, cutting him down.

He was dead.

All of a sudden, both of her phones started ringing.

Gasping, she jumped. She grabbed her cell phone to answer it. "Hello?"

No one was there.

Same for the office phone. All she heard was a dial tone.

"It doesn't hurt, you know."

She spun at the sound of a male voice behind her. It was the ghostly image of the man from the other building. "W-w-what doesn't hurt?" It was like someone else had control of her body. She was strangely calm and yet inwardly she was freaking out.

"Death. We all die." He walked through her.

Breathless, scared and shaking, she watched as he continued past her, to the wall. He went through it and walked back to his cubicle.

No... No...

No!

As soon as the ghost was over there, the corpse which was now lying on the floor turned its head toward her and smiled.

She stumbled back into the door.

Terrified, she spun around and clawed at the handle until she was able to open it.

Lesley met her on the other side. "Okay, you are seriously starting to freak me out. What's going on?"

I'm locked in a horror movie.

She didn't dare say that out loud. Les would never understand.

Without a word, she headed for the bathroom with her phone. She pulled up the email and then dialed the number.

"Hello?"

Wow, the exorcist sounded remarkably normal. Even friendly. "Is this Trisha?"

"Yes. You are..." she paused as if searching the cosmos for an answer. "Elliott Lawson."

"How did you know that?"

"I'm psychic, sweetie. I know many things."

Elliott wasn't so sure she liked the sound of that. But before she could comment, the phone went dead. She growled in frustration as she tried to dial it again.

Nothing went through.

Instead, her email filled up with more postings from Helga...

And other authors, too. Some of whom she hadn't worked with for several years.

"Why did you refuse to renew my contract?"

Elliott shrieked at the mousy voice that came out of a stall near her. A woman in her mid-thirties came out. Her skin had a grayish cast to it and her eyes were dark and soulless.

"Emily? What are you doing here?" Emily had been one of her first authors she'd bought as a new hire. They'd had a good ten book run before Elliott had made the decision to cut her from their schedule.

While Emily's numbers had held steady, they hadn't grown. Every editor was held accountable for their bottom line and Emily had been hurting her chances for advancement. So, Elliott had decided to move on to another author.

"Why did you do it? I was in the middle of a series. I had fans and my sales were growing. I don't understand."

"It was business."

Emily shook her head. "It wasn't business. I can count off three dozen other authors who don't sell as well as I did who you've kept on all these years."

"Not true." She always cut anyone who couldn't pull their weight.

Emily looked down at her arms, then held them up for Elliott to see. "I killed myself over it. After five years of us talking on the phone and working together, you didn't even send over a card. Not one stinking, lousy card for my funeral."

"I didn't know."

"You didn't care."

Elliott struggled to dial her phone. "You're not dead. This is a nightmare."

"I'm dead. Damned to hell for my suicide because of *you*!" Her eyes turned a bright, evil red as the skin on her face evaporated to that of a leather fleshed ghoul. She rushed at Elliott.

Screaming, Elliott ran for the door.

The handle was no longer there. She was trapped inside.

With Emily.

"Help me! Please! Someone help me!"

Emily grabbed her from behind and yanked on her hair. "That's what I begged for. Night, after night, after night. But no one answered my pleas either. I spent two years trying to get another contract and no one would touch me because of the lies you told about me. That I was hard to work with when I wasn't. All I ever dreamed about was being an author. I didn't want much. Just enough to live on. Two books a year. But you couldn't allow me to have even that much, could you? You ruined me."

"I'm sorry, Emily."

"It's too late for sorry." Emily slung her through the door.

Elliott pulled up short as she found herself back in her office. Only it was hot in here. Unbearable. She went to the window to open it.

She couldn't.

When she tried to turn the furnace down, it burned her hand. It whined before it spewed steam all over her.

She turned to run only to find more hateful notes from Helga.

Suddenly, laughter rang out. It filled the room and echoed in her ears.

She spun around, trying to locate the source. At first there was no one there. No one until Lesley appeared in the corner.

Elliott ran to her and grabbed her close, holding on to her like a lifeline. "I need to go home, Les. Right now."

"You are home, Elliott. This is where you spend all of your time. This is what you love. It's all you love." Lesley pulled out her chair and held it for her. "Go ahead. Reject those books. Crush more writers' dreams. You're famous for not pulling punches. For telling it like it is. Go on. I know how much you relish giving your honest, unvarnished opinion while never caring how much you hurt other people."

A thousand crying voices rang out in a harsh, cacophonous symphony.

Your writing is amateurish and pedestrian. Do not waste my time with anymore submis-

sions. I only give one per customer and your number is up.

If you can't take my criticism, then you've no business being a writer. Trust me. I'm a lot kinder than your readers, if you ever have any, will be.

While I found the idea intriguing, your writing was such that I couldn't get past the second page. I suggest you learn a modicum of grammar or better yet, stick to blog posts and twitter feeds for your creative outlet.

Over and over, she was inundated with rejections and comments she'd written to writers.

And for once, she realized just how harsh they were.

Elliott shook her head, trying to clear it. "Helga! Why are you haunting me? Why can't you leave me in peace?"

Lesley tsked at her. "Oh honey, Helga isn't haunting you."

"Yes, she is. I know I should have gone to her funeral, but—"

"Elliott, Helga didn't die." Lesley gestured toward her computer monitor. Her email vanished to show an image of Helga happily at work in her office. "*You* did."

"I don't understand."

Laughing, Lesley transformed into the

image of a red demon with glowing yellow eyes. "Welcome to hell, my dear. From this day forward and throughout all eternity, you will get to be Helga's editor. Oh, and I should mention, she's now doing a book a week."

Hell Hath No Fury

SHERRILYN KENYON

Chapter One

BASED ON A TRUE LEGEND

B*ased on a true legend*

"I don't think we should be here."

"Oh c'mon, Cait, calm down. Everything's fine. We have the equipment set and—"

"I feel like someone's watching me." Cait Irwin turned around slowly, scanning the thick woods that appeared to be even more sinister now that the sun was setting. The trees spread out in every direction, so thick and numerous that she couldn't even see where they'd parked her car, never mind the highway that was so far back nothing could be heard from it.

We could die here, and no one would know...

Her best friend from childhood, Anne, cocked her hip as she lowered her thermal imaging camera to smirk at Cait. "I hope something *is* watching you... Which direction should I be shooting?"

Cait shook her head at her friend's joy. There was nothing Anne loved more than a good ghost sighting. "Anne, I'm not joking. There's something here." She pinned her with a caustic glower. "You brought me along because I'm psychic, right?"

"Yeah."

"Then trust me. This..." Cait rubbed the chills from her arms, "isn't right."

"What's going on?" Brandon set his large camera crate down next to Anne's feet as he rejoined them. He and Jamie had gone out to set their DVR's and cameras for the night.

While she and Anne were slight of frame, Brandon and Jamie were well-bulked. Brandon more from beer and channel-surfing, and Jamie from hours spent in the gym.

Even so, with blond hair and blue eyes, Brandon was good-looking in a Boy Scout kind of way while Jamie had that whole dark, brooding sexy scowl thing that made most women melt and giggle whenever he glanced their way.

Anne indicated Cait with a jerk of her chin. "Wunderkind over there is already picking up something."

Brandon's eyes widened. "I hope you mean spirit-wise and not some backwoods bug we have no immunity to. I left my vitamin C at home."

Cait shivered as another wave of trepidation went through her. This one even stronger than the previous one. "Whose bright idea was this, anyway?"

Anne pointed to Brandon who grinned proudly.

He winked at her. "C'mon, Cait. It's a ghost town. We don't get to investigate one of these every day. Surely ye of the unflappable constitution isn't wigging out like a little girl at a horror movie."

"Boo!"

Cait shrieked as Jamie grabbed her from behind.

Laughing, he stepped around her, then shrugged his Alienware backpack off his shoulder and set it next to the camera case.

She glared at the walking mountain. "Damn it, Jamie! You're not funny."

"No, but you are. I didn't know you could jump that high. I'm impressed."

Hissing at him like a feral cat, she flicked her nails in his direction. "If I didn't think it'd come back on me, I'd hex you."

He flashed that devilish grin that was flanked by dimples so deep they cut moons into both of his cheeks. "Ah, baby, you can hex me up any time you want."

Cait suppressed a need to strangle him. All aggravation aside, a martial arts instructor who was built like Rambo might come in handy one day.

And still her Spidey senses tingled, warning her that that day might not be too far in the future.

"We're not supposed to be here." She bit her lip as she glanced around, trying to find what had her so rattled.

"No one is," Brandon said in a spooky tone. "This ground is cursed. Oooo-eeee-oooo..."

She ignored him. But he was right. At one time Randolph County had been the richest in all of Alabama. Until the locals had forced a Native American business owner to leave her store behind and walk the *Trail of Tears*.

"*Louina...*"

Cait jerked around as she heard the faint whisper of the woman's name- it was the same name as the ghost town they were standing in. Rather cruel to name the town after the woman who'd been run out for no real reason.

"*Louina,*" the voice repeated, even more insistent than before.

"Did you hear that?" she asked the others.

"Hear what?" Jamie checked his DVR. "I'm not picking up anything."

Something struck her hard in the chest, forcing her to take a step back.

Her friends and the forest vanished as she suddenly found herself inside an old trading post store. The scent of the pine board walls and floor mixed with that of spices and flour. But it was the scent of the soaps on the counter in front of her that was the strongest.

An older Native American woman, with her hair braided and coiled around her head, straightened the jars on the countertop while a younger pregnant woman, who had similar features, leaned against the opposite end.

But what shocked Cait was how much she favored the older woman. Right down to the black hair and high eyebrows.

The younger woman... Elizabeth. Cait didn't know how she knew that, but she did.

Elizabeth reached into one of the glass jars and pulled out a piece of licorice. "They're going to make you leave, Lou. I overheard them talking about it."

Louina scoffed at her sister's warning before she replaced the lid and pulled the jar away from her. "Our people have been here long before them, and we'll be here long after they're gone. Mark my words, Lizzie."

Elizabeth swallowed her piece of licorice. "Have you not heard what they've done to the Cherokee in Georgia?"

"I heard. But the Cherokee aren't the Creek. Our nation is strong. No one will touch us."

Elizabeth jerked, then placed her hand over her distended stomach where her baby kicked. "He gets upset every time I think about you being forced to leave."

"Then don't think about it. It won't happen. Not as long as I've been here."

"Cait!"

Cait jumped as Jamie shouted in her face. "W-what?"

"Are you with us? You blanked out for a second."

Blinking, she shook her head to clear it of the images that had seemed so real she could taste Elizabeth's licorice. "Where was that original trading post you guys mentioned being here?"

Brandon shrugged. "No idea. We couldn't find any information about it, other than it was owned by the woman the town was named for. Why?"

Because she had a bad feeling they were standing on it. But there was nothing to corroborate that. Nothing other than a bad feeling in the pit of her stomach.

In fact, there was nothing left of this once thriving town other than rows of crosses in a forgotten cemetery, and a marker that proclaimed it Louina, Alabama.

That thought had barely finished before she saw Louina again in her mind.

She was standing a few feet away to Cait's left with two wagons filled with as much money and supplies as she could carry. Furious, she spat on the ground and then spoke in Creek to the men who'd come to confiscate her home and store, and force her to leave.

Cait was sure it was Creek—a language she knew not at all—and yet the words were as clear to her as English.

"I curse this ground and all who dwell here. For what you've done to me... for the cruelty you have shown others, no one will make my business prosper, and when my sister passes from this existence to the next, within ten years of that date, there will be nothing left of this town except gravestones."

The sheriff and his deputies who'd been sent to escort her from her home laughed in her face. "Now don't be like that, Louina. This ain't personal against you. It's just business and all. We're just doing what the law tells us."

Louina curled her lips at him. "But it is personal against *you*." She cast a scathing glare to all of them. "No one will remember any of you as ever having breathed, but they will remember the name Louina and the atrocity you have committed against me. You will die forgotten, but I will always be remembered."

One of the deputies came from behind the second wagon with a stern frown. "Louina? This can't be all you own."

A cruel smile twisted her lips. "I couldn't carry all of my gold."

That piqued the deputies' interest.

"Where'd you leave it?" the sheriff asked.

"The safest place I know. In the arm's of my beloved husband."

The sheriff rubbed his thumb along the edge of his lips. "Yeah, but no one knows where you buried him."

"I know and I won't forget..." She swept a chilling gaze over all of them. "Anything."

And with that, she climbed onto her wagon and started forward without looking back. But there was no missing the smug satisfaction in her eyes.

She was leaving more than her store behind.

With every turn of the wheel, she cursed the prosperous town behind her.

Cait could hear Louina's malice as if it were her own thoughts. *They will tear each other apart, questing for the gold my husband will never release...*

It was Louina's final revenge.

One the eerie rows of cross-marked graves in the old Liberty Missionary Baptist Church Cemetery paid tribute to.

The weakness of our enemy is our strength.

Make my enemy brave, smart and strong, so that, if defeated, I will not be ashamed.

Cait felt Louina with her like her own shadow. A part of her she could only just see if the light hit it right.

Louina whispered in her ear, but this time she didn't understand the words.

Yet what was unmistakable was the feeling

of all-consuming dread that wouldn't go, no matter what she tried.

She sighed before she implored her group one more time. "We need to leave."

All three of them balked.

"We just got the equipment set out."

"What? Now? We've been here all day!"

"Really, Cait? What are you thinking?"

They spoke at once, but each voice was as clear as Louina's.

"We should not be here," she insisted. "The land itself is telling me we need to go. Screw the equipment, it's insured."

"No!" Brandon adamantly refused.

It was then that she understood why they were being stubborn when Brandon had spent his entire life proselytizing

that if you had a malevolent possession or haunting, you abandoned it. Because nothing was worth the chance of being possessed.

Only one thing would make him and Jamie abandon their beliefs.

Greed.

"You're not here for the ghosts. You're here for the treasure."

Jamie and Brandon exchanged a nervous glance.

"She *is* psychic," Anne reminded them.

Brandon cursed. "Who told you about the treasure?"

"Louina."

"Can she tell you where it is?" Jamie asked hopefully.

Cait screwed her face up at him. "Is that really all you're concerned with?"

"Well... Not *all*. We are here for the science. Natural curiosity being what it is. But let's face it, the equipment's not cheap and a little payback wouldn't be bad."

His choice of words only worsened her apprehension.

"Can you really not feel the anger here?" She gestured in the direction of the cemetery— that had been the first place they'd set up the equipment and it was there that her bad feelings had started. "It's so thick, I can smell it."

"I feel humidity."

Jamie raised his hand. "Sign me up for hunger."

"Annoyed," Brandon chimed in. "Look, it's for one night. Me and Jamie are going to dowse a little and try to find a place to dig."

How could he appear so chipper about what they were planning?

"You'll be digging up a grave."

They froze.

"What?" Brandon asked.

Cait nodded. "The treasure is buried with Louina's husband, William, who was one of the Creek leaders during the Red Stick War."

Jamie narrowed his gaze suspiciously. "How do you know all of this?"

"I told you. Louina. She keeps speaking to me."

Brandon snorted. "I'm laying money on Google. Nice try, C. You probably know where the money is and you're trying to scare us off. No deal, sister. I want a cut."

Laughing, Jamie chucked him on the back, then headed to the cooler to grab a beer.

Anne stepped closer to her. "Are you serious about this?"

Cait nodded. "I wish they'd believe me. But yeah. We don't need to be here. This land is saturated with malevolence. It's like a flowing river under the soil."

And with those words, she lost Anne's support. "Land can't be evil or cursed. You know that." She walked over to the men.

Cait knew better. Part Creek herself, she'd been raised on her mother's belief that if someone hated enough, they could transfer that ill spirit into objects and into the very soil.

Both were like sponges, and they could carry hatred for generations.

Louina was out there, and she was angry.

Most of all, she was vengeful.

And she's coming for us...

Chapter Two

Cait felt like a leper as she sat alone by the fire, eating her protein bar. The others were off in the woods, trying to summon the very entity she knew was with her.

"Louina?" Jamie called, his deep voice resonating through the woods. "If you can hear me, give me a sign."

While it was a common phrase, for some reason tonight it bothered her.

She mocked him silently as she pulled her wrapper down lower.

Suddenly, a scream rang out.

Cait shot to her feet and listened carefully to see who it was and where they were. Her heart pounded in her ears.

"Brandon!" Anne shouted, her voice echoing through the woods.

Cait ran toward them as fast as she could.

By the time she found them, Brandon was on his back with a twig poking all the way through his arm.

"He said he wanted a cut..."

She jerked around, trying to pinpoint the voice that had spoken loud and clear. "Did you hear that?" she asked the others.

"All I hear is Brandon whining like a bitch. Suck it up already, dude. Damn. You keep that up and I'm buying you a bra."

"Fuck you!" he snarled at Jamie. "Let me stab you with a stick and see how you feel. You the bitch. Asshole!"

"Boys!" Cait moved to stand between them. "What happened?"

"I don't know." Brandon hissed as Anne tried to see the wound. "I was walking, going over the thermal scan when all of a sudden, I stumbled and fell into a tree. Next thing I knew... this!" He held it up for her to see.

Cringing, Cait averted her eyes from the grisly wound. "We need to get him to the hospital."

"Not on your life," Brandon snarled. "I'll be all right."

"I take it back. You're not a bitch. You're insane. Look at the wound. I hate to agree with Cait 'cause I doubt there's a hospital anywhere near here, but you need help."

"It's a flesh wound."

Cait shook her head. "Anne, you should have never let him watch Monty Python."

"I should have never left him alone to go to the bathroom." Anne growled at him. "They're right. You need to see a doctor. You could get rabies or something."

Yeah, 'cause rabid trees were a huge problem here in Alabama.

Cait barely caught herself before she laughed. Anne hated to be laughed at.

"I'm not leaving till I find that treasure."

Greed, pride, and stupidity. The three most fatal traits any human could possess.

A sudden wind swept around them. This time, she wasn't the only one who heard the laughter it carried.

"What was that?" Jamie asked.

"Louina."

"Would you stop with that shit?" Brandon snapped through gritted teeth. "You're really getting on my nerves."

And they were getting on hers.

Fine. Whatever. She wasn't going to argue

anymore. It was their life. His wound. Who was she to keep him safe when he obviously had no interest in it?

Arms akimbo, Jamie sighed. "What do you think are the odds that, assuming Cait's right, Louina's husband has the gold in his grave that just happens to be in the cemetery? Didn't most of the Native Americans in this area convert over to Baptists?"

Cait shook her head. "He won't be there."

"What makes you say that?"

"If it was that easy to find, it would have been found."

"Yeah, good point. Square one sucks." Jamie glanced back to Brandon. "You sure about the doctor?"

"Positive."

"All right. I'm heading back out. Cait? You coming?"

"You can't go alone." She followed as he switched his flashlight on and went back to his EMF detector and air ion counter.

"You want to take this?" He held his full spectrum camcorder out to her.

"Sure." She opened it and turned it back on so that she could see the world through the scope of the small screen.

After few minutes, he paused. "Do you really believe any of the bullshit you've been spewing?"

"You know me, James. Have I ever spewed bullshit on site?"

"Nah. That's what has me worried." He narrowed his gaze at her. "Did I ever tell you that my great-grandmother was Cherokee."

"No, you didn't."

He nodded. "She died when I was six, but I still remember her, and something she'd always say keeps echoing in my head."

"What?"

"Listen, or your tongue will keep you deaf."

Cait was about to compliment her wisdom when she glanced down at the screen.

Holy Mother...

Gasping, she dropped the camera and jumped back.

"What?" Jamie turned around to see if there was something near them.

Terrified and shaking, Cait couldn't speak. She couldn't get the image out of her mind. She gestured to the camera.

With a stern frown, Jamie picked it up and ran the frames back. Even in the darkness, she knew the moment he saw what had stolen her tongue.

He turned stark white.

Right before he'd spoken about his Cherokee great-grandmother, a huge... something with fangs that appeared to be a ball of frenetic energy had been about to pounce on him. Soulless eyes of black had stared down as its mouth opened to devour him.

Then the moment he'd repeated the quote, it had pulled back and vanished.

Eyes wide, he gulped. "We have to leave."

She nodded, because she still couldn't speak.

Jamie took her arm gently and led her through the woods back to where they'd left Anne and Brandon.

They were already gone.

Jamie growled in frustration. "Brandon!" he called out. "Anne?"

Only silence answered them.

"All who dwell here will pay..." Louina's voice was more insistent now. *"But I hurt those I should not have cursed."*

Cait flinched as she saw an image of Elizabeth as an old woman in a stark hand-built cabin. Her gray hair was pulled back into a bun as she lit a candle and placed it in the window while she whispered a Creek prayer.

Oh, Great Father Spirit, whose voice I hear in the wind-

Whose breath gives life to all the world and with whom I have tried to walk beside throughout my days.

Hear me. I need your strength and wisdom.

Let me walk in beauty, and make my eyes ever behold the glorious sunset you have provided.

Make my hands respect the things you have made and my ears sharp to hear your voice even when it's nothing more than a faint whisper.

Make me wise so that I may understand the things you have taught my people. And why you have taken things from me that have given me pain.

Help me to remain calm and strong in the face of all that comes at me. Against my enemies and those out to do me harm.

Let me learn the lessons you have hidden in every leaf and rock. In the joy of the stream. In the light of the moon and sun.

Help me seek pure thoughts and act with the intention of helping others and never myself.

Help me find compassion without empathy overwhelming me.

I seek strength, not to be greater than my brother, but to fight my greatest enemy...

Myself.

Make me always ready to come to you with clean hands and straight eyes. So that when my life fades, as the fading sunset, my spirit may come to you without shame.

And most of all, Great-Grandfather, keep my sons safe and warm wherever they may be.

Elizabeth leaned over and kissed the old photographs of two young men in calvary uniforms that she had sitting in the window beside the candle she lit every night—just in case they finally found their way home. It was a ritual she'd practiced every single night for the last fifty-two years. Since the war had ended and her boys had failed to return home to tend their crops.

She refused to believe them dead. Just as she refused to die and let her sister's curse harm the town where they had both been born.

Her heart aching, Elizabeth pulled the last two brittle letters from her pocket that her boys had written to her and sat down at the table. Old age had taken her sight so that she could no longer read the words, not even with her spectacles. But it didn't matter. She'd long ago committed their words to her heart.

I dream only of returning home to marry Anabelle. Give her my best, Mother. Soon I will see you both again.

R.

He'd only been nineteen when he'd left her home with his older brother, John, when they'd been conscripted to fight a war that had nothing to do with them. Eighteen months older, John had sworn he would watch over Robby and return him home.

"On my life, Ecke. I'll bring him back whole and hale."

And I will watch for you every day, and every night I will light a candle to help guide you both to my door.

Tears swam in her eyes, but they didn't fall. She was stronger than that.

Instead, she reached for the old hand carved horn her father had given to her when she'd been a child. "Take this, Lizzie. Should anyone come to our door while your brothers and I are in the field, sound it loud to let us know and then hide with your mother and sisters until we can get to you."

So much had changed.

To this day, she didn't regret marrying her husband. She had loved her John more than anything. But he'd left her far too soon. She'd laid him to rest on a cold February morning when Robbie was barely seven. Since her brothers had been forced to leave along with her sister Lou, she'd raised the boys on her own, along with her daughter Mary.

There is no death, only a change of worlds...

Soon she would change. She could feel the Great Spirit with her more and more.

Do not grieve for that which is past or for that which you cannot prevent.

"I will see you again soon, my sons." And she would be with her Johns...

Cait flinched as she felt Louina's pain.

You must live your life from beginning to end. No one can do it for you. But be careful when you seek to destroy another. For it is your soul that will be consumed, and you are the one who will cry. Never allow anger and hatred to poison you.

"*I am poison...*"

Those words echoed in Cait's head as she followed Jamie in his quest to locate their friends.

"Maybe they went to the hospital, after all." That was her hope until they reached the tents they'd pitched earlier.

Tents that were now shredded and lying strewn across the ground.

Jamie ran ahead, then pulled up short. With a curse, he turned and caught her before she could get too close.

"You don't want to know."

"W-what?"

His gaze haunted, he tightened his arms around her. "Trust me, Cait. You don't want to see them. We have to call the authorities."

Tears welled in her eyes. "Anne?"

He shook his head. "It looks like an animal attack of some kind."

"Why!"

"I don't know."

But her question wasn't for Jamie. It was for Louina.

Words spoken in anger have strong power and they cannot be undone. For those who are lucky, they can be forgiven in time. But for others...

It is always our own words and deeds than condemn us. Never the ill intent or wishes of our enemies.

Do not dabble with what you don't understand. There are some doors that are blown from their hinges when they are opened. Doors that will never again be sealed.

"Welcome to my hell."

They both jerked at the voice beside them.

There in the darkness stood Louina. Her gray hair fanned out around her shoulders. Her old calico dress was faded against her white apron.

"My sister protects you. For that you should give thanks. Now, go and never come here again."

But it wasn't that simple.

"I won't leave and allow you to continue hurting others."

Louina laughed. "You can't stop me."

For the first time in her life, Cait understood the part of her bloodline that had always been mysterious and undefined. She was the great-great-granddaughter of Elizabeth.

It all came together in her mind at once. Her grandmother had told her the story of Elizabeth, who'd died when her cabin caught fire while she was sleeping. Something had knocked the candle that she lit for her sons from her window.

"You killed her!" Cait accused.

"She wanted to die. She was tired and it was time."

But that wasn't true, and she knew it. Yes, Elizabeth had been tired. She'd been almost a hundred and ten years old. Yet she'd been so determined to keep her sister's curse at bay that she'd refused Death every time it tried to claim her.

Until Louina had intervened.

In that moment, she felt a connection to Elizabeth. One she embraced.

Jamie released her. "What are you doing?"

Cait looked down to see the glow that enveloped her. Warm and sweet, it smelled like sunshine.

It was Elizabeth.

She embraced her like a warm hug.

"This ends, Louina. As you said, you are the poison that must be purged."

Shrieking, Louina ran for her.

True to her heritage, Cait stood her ground. She would not back down. Not in this.

Louina's spirit slammed into her with enough force to knock her down. She groaned as pain filled her.

Even so, she stood up and closed her eyes. "You will not defeat me. It is time for you to rest. You have not shown respect to those who dwell on this earth."

"They didn't show it to me!"

"And you allowed them to drive you away from the Great Spirit who loves us all. To do things you knew weren't right."

"They spat in my face."

"You returned their hatred with more." Cait reached her hand out to Louina. "Like

Elizabeth, you're tired. Nothing is more draining than to keep the fires of hatred burning."

"You will not fight me?"

Cait shook her head at her great-grandaunt. "I want to comfort you. It's time to let go, Lou. Release the hatred." And then she heard Elizabeth in her ear, telling her what to say. "Remember the words of Crazy Horse. Upon suffering beyond suffering, the Red Nation shall rise again, and it shall be a blessing for a sick world. A world filled with broken promises, selfishness and separations. A world longing for light again. I See a time of Seven Generations when all the colors of mankind will gather under the Sacred Tree of Life and the whole Earth will become one circle again. In that day, there will be those among the Lakota who will carry knowledge and understanding of unity among all living things and the young white ones will come to those of my people and ask for this wisdom. I salute the light within your eyes where the whole Universe dwells. For when you are at that center within you and I am that place within me, we shall be one."

Louina pulled back as she heard those words. "We are one," she repeated.

Elizabeth pulled away from Cait and held her hand out to Louina. "I have missed my sister."

"I have missed mine."

Jamie placed his hands on Cait's shoulders. "Are you all right?"

She wasn't sure. "Did you see any of that?"

"Yes, but I'm going to deny it if you ever ask me that in public."

Tears filled her eyes as she remembered Anne and Brandon. "Why did we come this weekend?"

"We came for greed. You came to help a friend."

Suddenly, a low moan sounded.

"Call for help," Jamie said as he released her and ran back to their camp.

She dialed 911, hoping it would pick up.

"Anne's still breathing." Jamie pulled his jacket off and draped it over her.

"What about Brandon?"

He went to check while the phone rang.

"It's faint, but yeah... I think he's alive too."

Cait prayed for a miracle she hoped would be granted.

Epilogue

C ait sat next to Anne's bed while the nurse finished checking her vitals. She didn't speak until after the woman had left them alone.

"Sorry we didn't have any readings to show you guys."

Anne shook her head. "Who cares? I'm just glad I'm alive. But..."

"But what?"

"Are you and Jamie ever going to tell us what really happened?"

Cait reached up to touch the small gold ring that she'd found on her car seat when she'd gone out to the road to help direct the medics to where Brandon and Anne had been.

Inside the band, the names John and Elizabeth were engraved. It was the only gold to be found in Louina.

And to her, it was priceless.

The treasure so many had sought had been used to fund a school and church over a century ago.

Years after her sister had given her the gold to support herself and her children, Elizabeth had taken the last of it and had it melted into this ring.

Smiling, Cait met Anne's gaze. "Maybe one day."

"And what about the treasure?"

"Anne, haven't you learned yet that it's not gold that is precious? It's people. And you are the greatest treasure of my life. I'm glad I still have my best friend."

Anne took her hand and held it. "I'm grateful to be here and I'm truly grateful for you. But—"

"There are no buts."

She nodded. "You're right, Cait. I'd lost sight of what my grandfather used to say."

"And that was?"

"When all the trees have been cut down and all the animals have been hunted to extinction, when all the waters are polluted and the air is unsafe to breathe, only then will you discover you cannot eat money."

Jamie laughed, drawing their attention to the door where he stood with a balloon bouquet for Anne.

"What's so funny?" Cait asked.

"I think we all came away from the weekend with a different lesson."

Cait arched her brow. "And that is?"

"Anne just said hers. You learned that revenge is a path best left alone. Brandon learned to shut up and get help when he's wounded."

"And you?" Anne asked.

"I learned two things. One, the most dangerous place for a man to be is between two fighting women. And two, no matter the species, the deadliest gender is always female. Men will fight until they die. Women will take it to the grave and then find a way back."

I-O-U

SHERRILYN KENYON

Chapter One

"Yeah, he's dead as a doornail."

Lucinda Fontaine gave her partner a droll stare as they stood across from a body that was pinned to a garage door by a giant spike through his chest. "You're not funny."

Sam Lopez grinned. "Sure, I am, cher. You just can't appreciate it."

Their lieutenant glared at both of them. "And I need both of you to be serious right now. We got reporters showing up, all over the place. Last thing I need or want is for any of them to start saying that Orleans Parish's finest is treating this matter with anything less than all due respect. You hear me?"

"Yes, sir," they snapped in unison.

"Good. Now get your gear on and don't be

contaminating my crime scene or compromising my evidence."

Lucinda pulled a pair of latex gloves out of the roll she kept clipped to her belt loop. She'd already put the plastic protectors on the bottom of her shoes. Something she'd learned to do as a rookie, since the last thing anyone wanted to do was track contaminates or evidence back into their car or home to their loved ones.

Covering her hair and face, she quickly set about examining the garage while the coroner and others did their job.

Sam stepped carefully around the broken glass on the ground so as not to slice through his shoe coverings. "Who called it in?"

"His wife. A uni is taking her statement inside." Lucinda sighed. "Apparently, she came home from work to find him like this."

"Alone?"

"It's what she said."

Sam frowned. "You believe her?"

Lucinda shrugged as she glanced up at the heavy-set man hanging from what appeared to be a piece of the garage door track that had somehow broken off and pierced him straight through his heart. "I don't think a four foot ten, ninety-pound Cajun woman could do that to him. She couldn't even reach that high standing on a ladder."

"Yeah, you got a point."

"And you call yourself a detective." Lucinda adjusted her mask as she leaned over to pick up a piece of crumpled paper. Straightening it out, it appeared to be a bill of some kind.

Sam came over. At five-six, he was almost even to her height. But in her tall rocker Sketchers, she had an inch on him. "What'd you find?"

"Credit card statement. Looks like he's been spending a lot of time at the casinos."

"And hotels." He pointed at the charges for the Hotel Monteleone.

"Fancy schmancy."

"Yeah, look at the amount."

He wasn't wrong. Strange for a man who lived locally to be spending that kind of dough for a luxury suite in the Quarter.

Lucinda listened idly at the chatter around them as her lieutenant walked past them. "Hey, boss? What you doing?"

"There's no need in keeping everyone on scene. This is an easy open-and-shut accident. I'm going to make a statement."

They were just beginning to pull the man

down from the wall when she and Sam headed inside to find the man's widow sitting on the couch.

Visibly shaken, the tiny woman sat with swollen eyes.

"I just can't believe this happened. I can't believe he's gone."

"Mrs. Marchand? Were you aware of your husband's gambling?" Lucinda wasn't sure why she felt the need to ask that when her boss had already closed the matter.

The tiny woman nodded. "Tony couldn't help himself. I knew it when I married him. It's how we met, in fact. I was a dealer at Harrod's." She looked up with a wistful smile. "What can I say? We both always liked to play the odds."

The doorbell rang.

"If you'll excuse me, that's probably my friend come to see if I'm all right."

Lucinda nodded.

Mrs. Marchand got up and walked off. The moment she did, the color faded from Sam's face.

"What's wrong?"

He glanced toward the door, then reached down into something that was partially buried in the woman's pocketbook and pulled it out.

"I might be crazy, after all, this is New Orleans. But really, what are the odds of this?"

In his hand, he held a voodoo doll that was dressed identically to the victim with a spike through its chest that held a note that read—*I-O-U.*

Karma

SHERRILYN KENYON

Chapter One

"He took my poppets."

Heather Anne looked up at her sister's deadpan voice. "Pardon?"

Elspeth took a deep breath as she walked calmly into the dark red bedroom where Heather Ann sat on her bed, watching her TV. Pausing at her footboard, she crossed her arms over her chest. "The fucking bastard stole my poppets."

Her jaw went slack at something that just wasn't done. While she'd known her sister was in the middle of a brutal divorce with an asshole of an ex, anyone with a brain knew you didn't steal someone's poppets.

Especially not those that were handmade

for them by a powerful maven. "Just how stupid is he?"

Elspeth gave her a pointed glare. At barely five feet in height and with dark brown hair, she was the spitting image of their mom. And that look made her insides shrivel.

She held her hands up in surrender. "Fair enough. I wouldn't want that mojo on me."

"Yeah." Ellie took the charm from her bracelet and removed it. "He's beyond redemption."

"Indeed." Harry had stolen all her money from her and walked out without a single word of warning to anyone. While he could have filed a simple divorce for irreconcilable differences and just halved their belongings like a normal human, he'd chosen to hire an absolute fucking moron of an attorney. One who'd accused her sister of every kind of madness from beating her six-foot-four coward of a husband who had been pampered and babied until it'd made Heather Ann sick . . . to witchcraft.

Effing nonsense.

The witch in the family had been their Aunt Birdie. The one who had made the poppets. Too bad she wasn't alive anymore. Birdie would have hexed him and made his tiny penis shrivel up and fall off.

And God help what she'd have done to his lying bitch of an attorney.

As it was . . .

"What do you think will happen?"

"I don't know. I guess it depends on if you believe Aunt Birdie's poppets have any power."

Heather Anne considered that. They were said to protect. When Ellie had first called her to say that Harry had run off, her first thoughts had been that the dolls must be working.

After all, Harry had been a spineless piece-of-shit husband. The kind who'd refused to work while he dabbled with his art career. Worse? The bastard had been cheating on her sister for years as her poor sister had worked three to four jobs to support him and their kids.

But since he'd spent the last two years dragging her sister and their young kids through the mud, and lying about them at every turn, she'd started to lose faith in those poppets.

Lose faith in everything.

Her sister had never done anything to that rank bastard. She was the last person to deserve the lies and abuse he'd heaped on her. Never mind all the lies and abuse from him and his jackal of an attorney and jealous girlfriend.

The injustice of it all had tested Heather

Anne's faith in everything and ruined her belief in the American court system that was obviously a rotting, useless joke.

Now . . .

"I hope those dolls work."

Ellie nodded.

Heather Anne scowled at her. "What are you doing?"

"Birdie always said that if something bad happened, I should take the charm she gave me and make a wish on it. I want that bastard dead! Him and his fucking whore of an attorney and girlfriend." She placed a kiss on the charm and put it into the box.

Heather Anne bit back a sarcastic snort. She wouldn't take this from her sister. Ellie had been put through enough. Besides, what would it hurt?

Someone needed to do something.

Sighing, she watched as Ellie taped the lid on the box and headed for her door.

"Goodnight, big sis."

"'Night."

* * *

Harry Chaddix sat alone in the house he'd stolen from his ex and those brats she'd birthed him. Pulling a beer from the fridge, he smirked as he glanced around the open kitchen and living room of what used to be her pride and joy. He'd gleefully lied so that he could rip it out from under her. God bless the stupidity of the modern court system and the vindictive judges who thought they were getting back at women for all the decades of the "poor" men who'd been abused at their hands.

He loved it.

"That's what you get, bitch. Told you what would happen if you ever tried to leave me. I'm the man! I'm the one in control. Not you! You can't have shit unless I say so!"

Laughing, he headed for the couch and picked up his remote. When he'd first moved in back when they married, this place had been packed with only her stuff. Gifts from fans and awards for her career. It sickened him. Why should he work when everything came so easy to her? She was a woman, and they were privileged. Let the bitch pay for his life.

For years, he'd been forced to stare at awards he'd known had only been given to her because she was female. Meanwhile, every time he'd tried to get anything off the ground, he'd failed. Because he was a man, and everything went to women.

It was sickening and he'd gladly thrown her shit out like the garbage it was.

Now . . .

He was never going to work again. The bitch could take care of him. It was what he deserved for putting up with her for twenty years.

"Harry?"

He pulled the beer from his lips. "What the fuck?"

No one was supposed to be here, but him. Getting up, he set his beer on the table.

"Harry?"

That sounded like Ellie's voice. "Bitch, you better not be here! I got a court order and I'll call the cops!"

He headed for the room that had been her office. It was now the bedroom where he jacked-off at night thinking of all the money of hers he was going to spend while making her beg him for mercy.

No one was there.

What the hell?

"Harry . . ."

He turned around slowly to see a shadow in the hallway where he'd just been.

A terrified chill went down his spine. "I'm

calling the cops, Ellie! You're not supposed to be here!" he repeated.

He went toward his bed only to remember the phone was on the kitchen counter.

Shit!

Fine, he could beat the bitch up. Wasn't like he hadn't done it before. She was half his size.

Furious, he headed for his phone.

No sooner had he left the bedroom than the door slammed shut behind him, and the lock he'd put on it to keep Ellie in buzzed to keep him out.

Panicking, he touched the doorknob.

It didn't move.

"Yeah, okay. It's just the wind."

But the ceiling fans weren't on.

"It's a mechanical failure."

Yeah, that had to be it.

His heart hammering, he swallowed and made his way down the short open hall. There was no one here. That was plain to see.

He was being stupid.

Suddenly, a droning heartbeat began to thump through the house speakers.

Like the *Tell-Tale Heart*. The bitch's favorite story . . .

"I'm not kidding, bitch! I'll kill you! I mean it!"

With a ragged breath, he had just reached the top of the stairs when he heard a whisper in his ear.

"You shouldn't take what doesn't belong to you." Then something shoved him from behind and caught his neck.

* * *

"You're not going to believe this."

Heather Anne looked up from her phone as she sat at her kitchen table, eating dinner.

Ellie was just coming in the backdoor from picking up her sons, who ran past, screaming for their gaming system. "What?"

"The police called me a few minutes ago."

Heather Anne groaned. "Ah, God. What bullshit lie has your bastard concocted now?"

"None. He's dead."

Her jaw went slack. "Pardon?"

"He died three days ago. Apparently, he hung himself in the house where he left a note."

"What did it say?"

"I'm sorry."

Heather Anne was stunned. "You're shitting me!"

She shook her head. "No and get this."

"What?"

"His attorney ran a red light today and slammed her car into his girlfriend's. They both died on impact."

The Neighbors

SHERRILYN KENYON

"I think there's something wrong with our neighbors." Jamie stepped back from the window to frown at his mom. "Have you seen them?"

"Just when the Thompsons moved in a few months ago and Teresa gave me her number."

"But not since, right? Isn't that weird?"

With long blond hair and bright green eyes that matched his, his mom picked up his little sister's backpack and set it on the table near him. "Not really. Teresa said that her husband's an international antique dealer. He travels a lot and keeps weird hours whenever he works from home."

Jamie moved to sit down at the table to do

his homework. "I'm telling you, Ma, there's something really, really off about them."

"Stop reading all those horror novels and watching those creepy movies and TV shows. No more *Dexter* on Netflix! It's all making you paranoid."

Maybe, but still . . .

Jamie had a bad feeling that wouldn't go away. Unsettled, he watched as his mom collected Matilda's toys and sighed from exhaustion.

It'd been hard for all of them over the last few months since his dad had been killed while off on a "business" trip.

As Jamie opened his chemistry book, a motion outside caught his attention. Frowning, he slid out of his chair to get a closer look.

He gaped at the sight of his neighbor carrying a strange-shaped baggie out of his detached garage and tossing it into the trunk of his car . . . which, now that he thought about it, was *never* parked *in* the garage.

Neither was Teresa's.

His neighbor struggled with the weight and odd shape of whatever was in the bag.

Was that a body?

C'mon, dude. Don't be stupid. It's not a body.

But Jamie had seen plenty of horror movies where they moved corpses, and that was what it looked like. It didn't even bend right.

"James? What are you doing?"

He pulled back to see his mom glaring at him. "Being my usual delusional self. You?"

"Wondering what I got into while pregnant that caused your brain damage. Must have been those lead paint chips I craved."

"Ha, ha." He returned to his homework, but as he tried to focus on chemistry, he couldn't get his mind off what he'd just seen. The way his neighbor had carried that bag . . .

It *had* to be a body.

Unable to concentrate, he got up to look outside again. The moment he did, he saw his neighbor's wife, Teresa, with a huge white bucket that held some kind of thick red liquid she was spreading around the driveway.

Red?

Water?

Nah, man. It was too thick for water. Looked like blood. Diluted maybe, but definitely a hemoglobin-like substance.

He started to call for his mom, but the moment he opened his mouth, Teresa looked up and caught sight of him in the window.

Terrified and shaking, he quickly hit the deck on his belly.

Oh God, she saw me!

What was he going to do? *I know what blood looks like. Even diluted.* And that had been blood she'd been dumping.

Maybe she's a taxidermist.

Yeah, right.

"Jamie?"

He flinched at his sister's call. Crawling across the floor, he didn't get up until he was in the hallway. "What'cha need, Matty?"

With honey-blond curls and bright blue eyes, his little sister stared up at him from the couch. "Can you come help me? I can't get the TV on the right channel."

"Sure." He moved toward her to check it out. The battery on the remote was low.

After changing it for her, he returned to the living room to put it on the kids channel she preferred, then froze as he heard the news.

"Another body was found near Miller's Pond. Mutilated. The headless remains were burned beyond recognition. At this time, the authorities are investigating every lead. So far, they're at a loss over this horrific crime that appears to be related to a set of six murders over the last four months."

Jamie froze to the spot as he heard those words.

"Give me that!" Matilda jerked the remote from his hand and changed channels.

Sick to his stomach, Jamie bit his lip. Now that he thought about it, those murders had only started after the Thompsons had moved in.

Six months ago. Just a few weeks after his father had been killed outside of Memphis.

Weird.

It's nothing, dumbass. Get back to your chemistry.

Yeah, but what if . . .

"Jamie?"

He turned at his mother's irate tone that usually denoted one bad habit he had. "I put the seat down!"

She growled at him. "It's not the toilet seat. I just got a call from Teresa. Are you spying on her?"

Well yeah, but he wasn't dumb enough to give her the truth with that tone of voice. "No."

Hands on hips, she glared at him. "You better not be! She said she's going to call the cops and report you for stalking if you do it again."

"'Cause I was looking out the window of my house? Really? When had *that* become a crime?"

"Don't get smart with me, boy. Now do your homework."

Grousing under his breath, Jamie returned to his book, but not before he texted his best friend.

By the time he'd finished his assignment, Ed was at his backdoor with an evil grin on his nerdy little face. Barely five-foot-three, Ed wasn't the most intimidating person on the planet, but he was one hell of an opponent on any science or math bowl team.

"So, you think your neighbors are weird."

"Shh." Jamie looked over his shoulder to make sure his mom wasn't there before he pushed Ed out onto the back stoop. "Yeah. There's something not right. You feel up to some snooping?"

"Always. It's what I do best. . . Only time my compact body mass comes in handy."

Ignoring his mini-tirade, Jamie turned the back light off and crouched low as he made his way from the porch to the grass. Like a military assault squad, they headed across his back yard, toward the Thompsons'.

Halfway to the Thompsons' garage, Ed pulled back with a frown.

"What?" Jamie whispered.

Blanching, Ed held his hand up for him to see. "It's blood." He looked around. "The ground's saturated with it."

Sick to his stomach, Jamie lifted his hands to see them stained red. Just like Ed's. "Is it human?"

"How would I know? Blood's blood. And this is definitely blood." Ed's eyes widened. "You think they're the serial killers the cops are looking for?"

"I don't know."

Biting his lip, Jamie moved toward the detached two-car garage to look for clues. It took several minutes to jimmy the lock.

As silent as the grave, he and Ed moved into the small building that was covered in plastic.

Like one of Dexter's kill zones.

Ed stepped closer to him. "We need to get out of here and call the cops."

"Not without some evidence."

"Yeah, no, I've seen this movie. Nerdy white boy dies first. I'm out of here."

He grabbed Ed's arm as his eyes adjusted to the darkness. "Hold on a minute."

Jamie went to the workbench where

someone had left a map of their small Mississippi town and a card case.

A card case that held driver's licenses.

What the hell?

Opening it, Jamie saw men and women from all over the country. *What kind of . . .*

His thoughts scattered as he saw his dad's license there.

Why would they have his dad's license?

Confused and terrified, Jamie looked back at the map that had his house and those of every family in town marked with a red highlighter.

"Jamie," Ed snarled between clenched teeth. "I hear something."

As they started back for the window, Jamie froze at the sight of a mirrored wall.

Footsteps moved closer.

Ed ran for the window with Jamie one step behind him. They were both sweating and shaking by the time they were outside the garage. But as soon as their feet were on the ground, headlights lit up the entire yard.

They were trapped.

If they tried to get back to Jamie's house, they'd be seen for sure.

With no other course of action, Jamie crouched under the open window and listened as the driver turned the car off and got out. Footsteps echoed as the driver walked into the garage.

"Hey, hon?" Mr. Thompson called out. "Have you been messing in the garage again?"

Lights came on in the house an instant before Teresa walked the short distance to the garage. "What?"

Ed ran for Jamie's house while Jamie stayed behind. Rising slowly, he peeked in through the mirror to see the Thompsons standing in the center of their obvious kill zone.

"Someone's been flipping through my journal. Was that you?"

"No. I haven't been in here." She walked over to the mirror.

Jamie gasped at what he saw there.

Oh shit! I knew it!

He lifted his phone and quickly snapped a photo of her, then he did what Ed had done. He scampered across the lawn as fast as he could. Running into his house, he slammed the door and pulled down all the windows.

"Mom!"

Ed met him in the living room where he was holding on to Matilda for everything he was worth. "I thought those things were myths made up by teachers and parents to scare us."

"What?" his mom asked.

Jamie swallowed as his mother stared at them as if they were crazy. His breathing ragged, he held his phone out to his mom. "We've got to call the cops!"

"For what?"

"Our neighbors, Ma!" He showed her the picture. "They're human . . . slayers. And they're here to destroy our colony!"

Toil & Trouble: A Dark-Hunter Hellchaser Story

SHERRILYN KENYON & MADAUG HISHINUMA

Chapter One

The eleventh bell rang out across the dismal shadows of Carrion Hill where three rigid, grey shapes practiced a dark, forbidden art. Yet it was one oft sought by those like the regal man standing before them, who'd shaken off his shackles of organized faith to beseech their wisdom and implore their sinister aid in his cause.

"Oh great Fates, with wisdom of old. Over your cauldron, where you toil. I beseech you now, for your gifted sight. To carry me forward through this night. What will come, good or foul? This I must know, before dawn's first prowl."

He held himself with the familiar arrogance the witches didn't need their single eye to see.

Rich robes fashioned from hues of red, orange, and purple that had been woven by the hands of those he deemed unworthy and trimmed with gold thread until those same poor women had gone blind from their imposed labors.

Now he, the feared master, came to them as a loyal servant to offer minted gold and jewels to the witches three to whom he bowed in utmost respect. And well he should. For they were the shapers of destiny. Older than time and more callous than any king.

Dieno the sister who had the ability to see every tragedy lurking within a single lifetime. That was her gift.

It was also her curse.

Enyo's visions showed the battles that awaited their querent. Small and large. Every skirmish, every death match. She could tell this one exactly who was plotting against him.

And last was their petite sister, Persis, whom others cruelly mocked as "the destroyer" for she knew the steps one could take to avoid their fate . . .

Or cause it. Her words about the future were the ones that mattered most. They were the guidance that could make or break a single life.

The irony was that everyone knew it and

yet failed to listen, time and again. But that was because these Stygian witches were missing their fourth sister, Pemphredo. She'd been the one who could show their querent the way through their prophesies. The one who could guide them to safety and unravel their verse.

Without her . . .

Humans were screwed.

Since time immemorial the witches of Carrion Hill had foretold and guided the destiny of lord and pauper alike. King and peasant. In their hands lay the power to destroy nations—to shatter dynasties . . .

Or save souls.

'Twas this power that made them the sole arbiters of truth in a time and land dominated by chaos.

"Listen!"

"Hear!"

"See!"

The witches spoke out, one by one. As they'd rehearsed a thousand times before. The sisters cackled and howled, and prepared their boiling cauldron. They threw in the usual, expected ingredients as they didn't want to disappoint their customer—eye of newt, wing of bat, and the withered tongue of a liar . . . all humanely gathered, naturally, as the sisters were ever conscious and respectful of such concerns. The last thing they'd ever want was to insult anyone's sensibilities, as that had nefarious endings for their kind, such as causing them to end up tied to stakes and set on fire.

Or thrown into ovens by ungrateful, bratling children they'd taken in after their parents had thoughtlessly lost them in the woods.

People were ever vicious that way. And every year more and more of their sisters were lost to such cruelty. Soon it would be just them and Uzarah left to guard the gates if things didn't change. Then mankind would know why witches had been necessary in this world.

Not to practice magic or foretell silly fortunes for those too weak to make their own fate.

They were here to cast back into darkness the mistakes the gods had made. To shield mortals from their own stupidity and incessant need to fabricate their destruction.

But they, like humanity, were growing old and tired. And with every sniveling request such as this, the sisters three really didn't see a need to salvage this world or the ones who wasted their time with such trivialities as their own fortunes when the entire universe set poised on the verge of annihilation.

As the ingredients simmered, they stirred the pot three times, one for each of them, and muttered their time-honored chants.

"Double, double. Toil and trouble.

"Fire burn, and cauldron bubble.

"For a charm of powerful trouble,

"Like a hell-broth boil and bubble.

"Come and see. Come what may.

"Things we want and things to delay."

Now came the fun part . . . Magic was more art than science and while Deino saw the trouble that lurked ahead and Enyo heard the battles to come, it would be up to Persis to give him the words he needed to avoid those catastrophes.

Not that it would matter. Mortals never listened. They were ever bent on their own destruction.

Dieno scooped up her Stygian eye from the cauldron in order to look into the prophecy taking form. There, she could see the man's fate in motion while her grey sisters could hear it—a vicious cycle which would continue for a hundred generations.

One that was older than the icy hand of time . . . a foolish family would cast out their own. Despondent and angry, he'd take his revenge upon them in a brutal series of murders, only to be brutally murdered by his own children in turn.

Round and round, the hatred grows.
Killing all kindness everywhere it goes.
Where it stops . . .
Well, we know.

And they could tell him, but what was the fun in that?

Enyo pursed her lips. "Not the most original of prophecies, is it?" she whispered.

Persis sighed as she grabbed the eye for her own look. "Nay. Seems as if patricide be the crime of the hour. How very gauche."

"Can't they ever come up with something more original? Like pinning cheese to their balls?" Deino retook the eye, trying to find a better outcome.

Same old, same old.

In spite of their steadfast denials, people were seldom original.

After a lifetime of predicting brutal tragedies that ended with such karmic deaths any perpetrator with half a brain should have guessed would happen, the witches had grown so very bored with it all.

How many ways could they say the same thing?

Don't be an idiot. Nay, really, stop being stu-

pid. Don't . . . you will hurt yourself.

Still, they persisted. It was as if humanity wanted to bleed.

Worse, they wanted to whine.

Case in point. Such a simple prophecy. One that could be easily avoided by giving the child a loving home. If only the father would do so. But as with Oedipus and his father, Laius, he wouldn't listen to their wisdom.

How many times would they waste their collective breaths? Why did he even bother to come here when he had no intention of hearing them?

"Double, double. Toil and trouble.

"Fire burn, and cauldron bubble.

"Humans come and humans die.

"'Me life's unfair,' they always cry."

The sisters took a moment to discuss what they would tell this wretched mortal.

"No need to speak the truth," Enyo whispered.

"Shall we make a bet?"

Deino liked where her sister went. "Aye!" She cracked a rare smile as they began to think in verse.

The rules of their species forbid them to ever give their sight outright.

Clearing her throat, she lifted the eye so

that she stared out at the arrogant man in all his finery. "Here your future for to see,

"Clad in darkness, he brings misery.

"A hundred swords light a hundred fires deep,

"And at the knees of each soldier doth a maiden weep.

"Over and over, a kingdom is lost.

"Such a horrid, dreadful cost.

"For in the end, the answer's clear . . .

"Be careful of the evil you hold so dear."

The man scowled at their prophecy as if he were baffled by it.

Deino stifled her smile. She could tell he was frightened by his bleak future. And well he should be. Even so, he mustered a polite bow and thanked them for their time, then paid them well.

"Good riddance." Enyo lowered the hood from her cloak and extinguished the fire. They were done for the night.

"Was it right? What you did?"

They paused at the sound of their apprentice. Eeri was a little snipe of a thing who constantly stuck her nose where it didn't belong. She pretended to have the good of others in her heart, but even blind, Deino could see through the little blonde's treachery.

"Clean out the cauldron."

Eeri watched as the three witches hobbled off to sleep and glared at their departing backs. How she loathed them. They were the worst.

She should know. Her own parents had sold her off to them for nothing more than a bag of grain when she'd been a child. And she'd hated them every moment since. Imagine, being worth nothing more than a sack of seed.

"Bitches brew," she snarled at their fetid concoction before she spat into it. The bubbling liquid hissed, then a green cloud shot up, toward the sky.

Her eyes widened in terror as she feared they might see what she'd done and harm her for it. They could be incredibly cruel over such things.

Best not to try her luck with them.

Swallowing hard, she quickly set about cleaning up. After all, she had a big day ahead of her tomorrow. The last thing she wanted was to be sleepy or tired.

* * *

The next morning, Eeri made her monthly trek to town to purchase supplies for her witch mistresses. These were the days she loved best of all, as they gave her a break from the three Stygian bitches and their sing-songy lies. She didn't believe in anything they said. How could she? It was always vague nonsense that could apply to anyone.

Anything.

Screwing her face up, she mocked their prophecy from the night before. "Here your future for to see,

"Clad in darkness, he brings misery.

"A hundred swords light a hundred fires deep,

"And at the knees of each soldier doth a maiden weep.

"Over and over, a kingdom is lost.

"Such a horrid, dreadful cost.

"For in the end, the answer's clear . . .

"Be careful of the evil you hold so dear." She scoffed, then snorted. "Utter rubbish, I say. Me farts hold more prophecy than that . . . smell better too than that shite them witches brew."

Letting out a tired breath, she stared up at the bright blue sky. "I'd give aught to be done with the lot of them!"

All she'd ever wanted was to belong to someone. Belong to something like this quaint little village, celebrating the vernal equinox—a time for new beginnings. How she wished she could be one of them. Cheery and friendly, and free of the Stygian three.

Depressed, she walked past bright colors that shot out from open doorways while the townspeople excitedly drank and danced in their revelry. All around, laughter came at her, yet she felt none of it.

Not that it mattered. This was a good atmosphere for fortunetelling. Just as she'd known it'd be. Those around her would make good prey . . . er, practice for her future trade.

Her spirits perking up at the thought, Eeri pulled out the small crystal ball she'd packed and looked about for a place to set up a makeshift stand.

Not too dark or drab. Inviting and promising.

Unlike the bitches in the woods.

They were pathetic and old. And since the day she'd been bought, it'd been her dream that someday, with enough money, she could purchase her freedom from those old heifers. That was all she wanted. A life apart from creatures like them.

Sadly, she had to deal with them. So, she made sure to gather their ingredients first lest she, by way of her body parts, become part of their apothecary.

Then, she found a nice corner in the marketplace to set up a makeshift table for her ball.

Within minutes a couple came by and sat across from her.

Finally!

"Tell me about my future." The man smiled and handed off a dirty coin.

Eeri could smell the alcohol on him, but he seemed pleasant enough.

The girl at his side gave her a sheepish grin. "I know he doesn't look his best right now, but it's a festival, you know? Anyway, are we meant to be?"

Eeri suppressed a shiver. God save her from that fate. Yet who was she to cast dispersions on the woman's ambitions?

One woman's rose, another's asshole.

With a deep breath, Eeri moved her hands around the ball, calling on the powers of beings from beyond to show her the weave of the universe.

If their life forces were entwined.

She saw the man before her drinking heavily as burly men looted his home.

The woman by his side wasn't happy.

Rather she sat with dejected, dead eyes as the men raided her meager possessions.

A stout man hefted a heavy axe over his shoulder. "This be why you don't go a' gambling, worm. The Lord giveth and we taketh." He cut off the man's hand.

She grimaced at the nightmare, then met their eager gazes. A horrible future easily corrected without verse or the boiling of oats or toads. "Beware your gambling and heavy drinking in the future if you want to remain together and whole."

The woman let out a gleeful cheer as she shot to her feet. Quickly, she grabbed him up and dragged him away.

As they vanished into the crowd, Eeri could hear her letting him have it about his drunken tendencies.

There now. That was how you told a prophecy!

She spent the rest of the day dispensing similar fortunes. They were all simple people with simple lives, but she would have it no other way.

Yet all too soon, the sun set and the night grew cold. A chilly breeze sought to drive her from the village, back into the woods and up the hill. Even so, she'd made a pretty penny and it was time to retire for the night and bring her ingredients home.

As she was packing her ball, she felt a peculiar presence near that caused the hair on her arms to stand on end.

Until then, she hadn't noticed that the night had become unbearably quiet. No sound could be heard. Not even the barking of a dog.

Only her heartbeat in her ears.

Until the sound was overtaken by the heavy footfall of a stranger. The sound grew louder with every step as he came closer and closer still.

A figure wrapped in utter darkness, walking straight toward her.

She wanted to run.

Needed to run. But fear had paralyzed every muscle in her young body until the stranger was upon her.

Tall and muscular, he had the swagger of a warrior and the confidence of a king. This man was legendary.

Without breaking stride, he took a seat at her makeshift fortuneteller's table. Still wrapped in silence, he pulled out a blood-stained invitation and dropped it beside her hand.

She gulped audibly. What he held was rare,

indeed. A favor card given by the witches to someone who'd once gone out of his or her way to pay them a kindness.

It meant that the bitches now owed him a favor in turn.

Those cards they hoarded more closely than gold as they never wanted to be beholden to anyone.

Who was this man?

She was desperate to know. Yet she could see no trace of any feature. It was as if all light avoided him. As if it cringed from him. All she could make out was a subtle sneer in his dark visage.

He tapped his card three times and her senses returned. As frightening as the man was, he must be close friends with the witches on the Hill. Only one of those rare breeds would have such a card.

So, she dug out her crystal ball to tell one last fortune for the night.

Cradling it like a babe, she moved her hands over the ball. She saw the man standing proudly next to a flaming pile of dead witches.

A lot of dead witches.

"Witchkiller," Eeri breathed.

With a cruel smile, he leaned closer like a predator before his prey.

Her heart pounding, she yelped and knocked the table over. She heard her prized ball shatter against the cobblestone road as she sent the witches' supplies scattering.

Nothing mattered to her at the moment, except saving her own life.

He was evil!

Death!

Terrified, she ran as fast as she could, and dared not look back in fear that the man would catch her.

I have to warn the others! She might hate them, but no one deserved the deaths she'd seen.

By the time she reached the small cottage, she was shaking and weak.

No one had caught her. Thank the old gods!

Relief poured through her.

Until she heard the laughter from inside.

She peered through a window and saw Enyo seated before the fire, playing a game of chess with Deino. Safe and warm, the sisters were recounting tales of the kingdoms they'd seen crumble in their prophecies.

Life's not fair.

Righteous anger filled her. Why should they have a family when she had no one? She'd never harmed anyone and yet here she was, alone, in the dark, being threatened, while they laughed and carried on in peace and warmth.

Let them die!

They deserved it. It would serve them right. After all, she'd been gone for hours and they weren't even looking for her. For all they knew, she was dead, like the others.

And did they care?

Not a bit.

So, why should she warn them?

Let him have them and you're free.

What she had always wanted. Who would know?

Licking her lips, she glanced about. It was true. She knew where Enyo had money hid. It would be enough to see her through.

Aye, this was her chance . . .

Freedom!

Stealthily, she crept away from the cottage and back into the woods.

"I will find you, money mine.

"And we'll be together for all time."

After all, that was the only thing she really needed. Her money had been lost in the village. She'd been so startled by the man that she'd left it behind. So, it was only right and fair that she take from the sisters.

They deserved it.

"Help! Help! I'm caught in a trap."

Eeri froze at the masculine voice. No one should be in the woods tonight. But there was no mistaking the man. She wanted to ignore him, but the bastard was in her way. There would be no way to leave without his seeing her.

And she remembered the card.

A favor for a favor. Mayhap if she saved him, he'd help her escape the Witchkiller. She didn't know how to fight, but this man might.

So, she followed his calls until she found him hidden in a small copse of trees. A hand-some, beautiful man in the prime of his life with dark-blond hair and glowing green eyes.

Caught in a bear trap, he hissed and snarled as he tried to get himself loose.

"Hello?"

He righted himself at her voice and turned to face her.

Startled, she realized that he was dressed just as the man she'd seen earlier. Same black clothes and lethal aura. Yet not quite as blood-thirsty.

His peculiar gaze swept over her body, making her instantly aware of how unap-pealing she appeared. Covered in dirt and grime, she dripped with enough sweat that he could probably smell her from his distance. Her long blond hair had come loose of its braid to tumble around her thin shoulders. He must think her hideous.

But instead of cringing, he laughed. "I'm glad to see someone is faring worse than I." His laughter ended in a hiss of pain.

"Hold still." She went to bend down next to him.

Ugh! The trap was so tightly clamped around his leg that she couldn't budge it. All she did was hurt him more.

After the third time of her clamping it more tightly to his ankle, she wrinkled her nose at his pain-filled grimace. "I'll go get help."

But she didn't.

As soon as she was clear, her common sense returned, and she remembered that he wore the same suit as the man who was out to kill everyone like her.

He was her enemy.

Do unto others before they do unto you!

Aye, better he should die than should she.

And so she ran away from the village and the Carrion Hill. Just as hard and fast as she could.

Or so she thought.

Confused, Eeri came upon a village that looked strangely familiar.

Nay, it was familiar! And it was crowded with others dressed just like the man from her table and the one she'd left to die.

Men holding swords . . .

She started to turn away, but something wouldn't let her. An unseen force kept her there, then suddenly, it felt like her soul had been ripped from her body.

What is happening?

The man in black appeared in the crowd. They parted so that he could walk through them and climb to a small platform and speak for the first time. "I stand before you, not above.

"Never plotting against those you love.

"Speak no evil, not in life.

"Never tarry and cause no strife.

"Yet they stand above us mortal men.

"Plotting against us at their whim.

"We are helpless against their guile.

"Until we're choking on our bile.

"But no more sway will they hold.

"And no more lies will be told.

"Brothers, sisters, is this not what I promised you?

"That there are those who will get their due?

"Savage ends for savage beasts.

"Come tonight, we shall feast!

"Fetch your torches, sword and all.

"A hundred witches tonight will fall!"

Gasping, Eeri turned and almost ran straight into the man she'd left in the woods.

He tsked at her. "With Ate by his side come hot from hell. Shall in these confines with a monarch's voice cry 'Havoc!' and let slip the dogs of war, that this foul deed shall smell above the earth."

"Beg pardon?"

He laughed at her question. "You can beg all you want, little one. But you judged your sisters for your crimes and for that you are damned."

"I don't understand."

Thorn stepped back so that she could see her table, toppled and littered with the sisters' supplies.

And there lay her body beside it.

"You didn't escape the Carrion beast. Nor did you pass my test." Shaking his head, he looked to the hill, now ablaze from the horde. "Come, Misery. I have a place where you belong."

Devil's in the Details

SHERRILYN KENYON

Chapter One

"**B**e careful. The devil will steal your soul."
        Shifting the heavy cardboard box in her arms,

Anna Carol blinked at the ominous voice. "Excuse me?"

No one was there.

A chill went up her spine as she turned around slowly in her new apartment and glanced at the empty white walls surrounding her.

Nothing.

It looked as cheery and bright as it had two weeks ago when the plump little real estate lady had led her through it, and she'd fallen in love with the place. It'd only taken her fifteen minutes to decide that this was where she wanted to start her life over. That this was the right place to begin fresh.

Richmond, Virginia. Childhood home of Edgar Allen Poe. The place where Patrick Henry had delivered his infamous "Give Me Liberty or Death" speech. This was where they'd passed the first statute for Religious Freedom written by Thomas Jefferson.

At one time, Virginia was America. This was where it'd all begun. Decades before the Pilgrims had made landfall at Plymouth Rock, the colonists in Virginia had intrepidly carved out new lives for themselves here in the wilds off the banks of the James River.

So, it was ironic that when Anna had dragged out the old road map her father had once used to plan holiday fishing trips, closed her eyes, and randomly placed a thumbtack on a city to move to after her divorce, it had landed squarely on the very city that one of her own ancestors had boldly helped to build.

It still gave her a chill whenever she thought about it.

Having decided that she was going to pick up everything and go wherever fate decreed, here she was.

Richmond.

No regrets.

If only she could say as much about her marriage.

Don't think about it. Rick was a prick. That was her motto.

She couldn't change her past. Only her attitude about it. And so, she'd sold everything she could, packed up her red Jeep Wrangler, and hightailed it from Huntsville to Richmond.

To start over. Tabula rasa.

It certainly didn't get more blank or Spartan than this apartment with its plain, white walls that stared at her with threatening austerity.

She shivered in revulsion, wishing she could paint them the bright eggplant and green colors she'd used in her old Huntsville house. The house Rick had managed to steal out from under her.

Along with her dignity. Friends.

He'd even taken her cat.

Bastard!

"I'll get some pictures." Some drapes.

That would help cheer things up a bit more. Especially if one was a picture of her ex with an axe planted firmly between his eyes.

Smiling at the thought, Anna set the box down, then opened her door to return to her car for another load . . . and almost ran smack dab into a young man.

Handsome and ripped, he was dressed in shorts and a t-shirt as if he were about to go running.

"Oh, sorry," he mumbled. "I wasn't paying attention."

She scowled as she caught a glimpse of his pupils through his dark sunglasses. For an instant, she could have sworn they flashed red.

Must have been an optical illusion.

"No problem. I'm just moving in."

"Ah." He glanced at her door. "I'm in the apartment above you. I was wondering if anyone would ever move into this one, again."

Her frown deepened at the odd note in his voice. "What do you mean?"

He stopped scrolling through his playlist and lowered his phone. "You hadn't heard?"

She squelched a shiver at his ominous tone. "Heard what?"

One brow shot north. "Um . . . nothing. Nothing at all." As he started to leave, she stopped him.

"Do you have a name?"

"Of course." And with that, he dodged out the doors and down the stairs, toward the parking lot.

Okay, then. He'd obviously flunked Southern Hospitality 101 and taken an extra course in Rude.

"Ignore, Luke. He has a personality disorder."

She turned toward the stairs behind her to find an impressive, short, voluptuous brunette standing there in a pair of ragged jeans and a black tee.

Was there some unwritten law that everyone in her building had to be extremely attractive?

And a little creepy.

Anna wondered how she'd made the cut, given the fact that she was twenty pounds over-weight and approaching middle age at warp speed. Not to mention, she was hot and sweaty, and unlike her neighbors, her sweat didn't make her glisten.

It made her gross and smelly.

"Which Alphabet Soup label does he fall under?" Anna asked the beauty as she came closer.

"TAS."

Anna scratched at the sweat on her cheek. "Never heard of it."

"Terminal Asshole Syndrome. Not sure if it was congenital or something he contracted after puberty. Either way, he has a fatal dose of it."

She laughed at the woman. "I'm Anna Carol, by the way."

"Two first names? Or did God not like you to curse you with that particular moniker."

"The latter."

"Ouch. Not that the Big Guy or mi querida madre was any kinder to me." She tucked her hands in to her jeans pockets. "Marisol Verástegui."

"That's beautiful."

"Glad you think so. But then you're not the one who has to try and get it straight at the DMV, or on any legal document. Talk about a nightmare!"

"I can see where that might make you crazy."

"Oh yeah. But hey, it's hysterical at Starbucks. I love to make the baristas cry."

Anna laughed. While Luke might leave a lot to be desired in the friendly department, she really liked this neighbor. "It's nice to meet you, Marisol. I take it you live upstairs, too?"

"I used to." A dark sadness came into her eyes.

"Used to?"

Marisol nodded, then turned around and walked through the wall.

Anna choked on a scream.

The entire backside of Marisol's skull was missing.

Chapter Two

"You can't break your lease, Ms. Carol. It's impossible."

Anna gripped her phone tighter. Over the last two weeks, she hadn't slept, or had a moment of peace. The hauntings that had begun with Luke—who turned out to be a suicide from three years ago, and Marisol who'd died in a murder last year—had only gotten worse and worse.

"Of course, I can. Just tell me how much."

The realtor let out a low, sinister laugh that didn't sound like her usual high-pitched voice. "You don't understand. You entered the agreement of your own volition. No one forced you into it. The moment you did so, you became one of ours."

One of who? What?

"Pardon?"

"You heard me. You came to me seeking a new life. I delivered it. You have a new job and a place to live. I fulfilled our bargain. In return, you signed away your soul."

Seriously, this had to be a joke. Was the realtor high?

"Um . . . what?"

"You heard me," Annabeth Lawrence repeated. "Read the fine print on the contract. You came here looking to start over. I told you when I handed you the keys, and you crossed the apartment's threshold that you would be entering a whole new life. Did you think I was kidding?"

"I assumed you were speaking metaphorically."

"Well, you know what they say about assume. It makes an ass out of u and me." Then, the witch had the nerve to actually hang up.

Hang up!

Demonic laughter rang through her apartment.

Unamused, Anna stood there, grinding her teeth.

Okay. I have sold my soul to the devil.

She had no response to that. Face it, it

wasn't exactly something someone dealt with every day.

At least not normal people.

"Well, it's a good thing I come from a basket load of crazy."

And that was being generous. Crazy had kind of looped around her family a couple of times, rebounded back, decided it really liked them, and then moved in and planted some serious roots. Then, because she was really Southern, it had remarried a few cousins, committed incest, and decided to never branch off her family tree. So, the lunacy had just quadrupled with each subsequent generation until it was no longer eccentric, it was downright felonious.

Yeah, that was her family.

And that was her insanity.

In Randolph County, Alabama, where her family hailed from, she could get someone killed for a simple keg of beer.

No questions asked.

Which was why she'd moved to Huntsville when she married. Although her ex had often claimed that three hours away just wasn't far enough.

Sometimes, she agreed.

But right now, she needed that kind of

crazy, because they were the only ones who could make *this* seem normal. Not to mention, they were the only ones who wouldn't have her committed when she called them.

Anna started to dial her father, then stopped herself.

After all, she *was* in Satan's apartment.

Um, yeah. She'd seen enough horror movies to know how this would play out. It always ended the same for the idiot on the phone.

Grisly death.

Usually some dismemberment.

Deciding that she liked her body parts in their current locations, Anna slid her phone into her back pocket. "I'm just going to the grocery store to get some milk. I'll be back in a minute."

Last thing she needed was for the entities here to think she was going to do something underhanded . . .

Like call in reinforcements.

As calmly as she could, she grabbed her keys and pocketbook, then headed for the door. "Hey, Satan? Could you turn out the lights for me? Thanks!"

She headed outside and tried not to freak over the fact that as soon she got into her Jeep, and looked back at her apartment, she saw the lights turn off.

By themselves.

Never let it be said that the devil didn't have a wicked sense of humor.

Trying to stay calm, she quickly belted herself in and drove to the store as if all was right in the world (and her mind). Just in case she had an unseen visitor keeping her company.

She'd seen that movie, too.

Once she was inside the store and had found a place where nothing too hard or sharp could fall on her, and where she had a good line-of-sight on anyone who might get possessed and come charging after her, including devil or zombie dogs, rats or insects, she dialed her dad.

No, there's nothing wrong with me, doctor. Really. I've always been a little touched.

Anne snorted at her thoughts as the phone rang.

Luckily, her father wasn't out bowling with his buds or watching a game. He never picked up the phone on game nights.

"Hey, pumpkin pie. How's my girl?"

"Hey, Daddy. I have a little problem." She glanced around the store and lowered her voice so that no one could overhear her and think her nuts. 'Cause honestly, she thought she was pretty crazy herself. "Turns out, you've been wrong in your sermons lately. The devil isn't coming up in those hell-pits down in Georgia that's been causing their interstates to rise up and buckle. He's actually here in Richmond. Living in my apartment building."

"Say what?"

"Uh, yeah. Apparently, I accidentally sold my soul to him when I signed my lease."

Now most fathers would probably have committed their daughters over such a statement. At the very least, would have laughed it off, and thought it a prank.

Lucky thing for Anna, her daddy was a Southern Baptist preacher who specialized in spiritual warfare. In fact, her family came from a long, long line of men and women who were famed for scaring the devil out of generations of parishioners and farms.

Even livestock and the occasional gentleman suitor who thought to come calling on their daughters.

And one old rusted-out moonshine still from back in the days of Prohibition when it'd supposedly gotten possessed by an angry demon who was running amok in an Ap-

palachian hill town . . . but that was another
story.

The good news was that when it came to
things like this, her father didn't blink an eye.

But he did rush to action, and he always
took it seriously.

"All right, baby girl. You know what to do.
The cavalry's coming. You hold tight and we'll
be there by morning."

No words had ever sounded sweeter.

"Thank you, Daddy!" Normally, it would
take about nine-and-a-half hours to make the
drive from where her daddy lived in Wedowee
to her apartment in Richmond. But given her
dire circumstances, and her father's propensity
for ignoring the posted limitations on speed
and his lack of needing to go to the bathroom
on long trips, she'd expect him in about seven.
Maybe six.

Her daddy was awesome that way.

And she knew he wouldn't bother to pack.
He always kept a bug-out sack of clothes and
his exorcism bag in his old Army HMMWV for
just such emergencies (or a zombie apocalypse,
'cause one could never be too careful).

Yeah, Old Scratch had no idea what he was
in for.

Then again, given that the devil had supposedly gone a few rounds with her father in the past, he probably did.

And for once, the demons had picked the wrong person to muck with.

Smiling, Anna started back for her Jeep in the parking lot, then remembered that she actually did need milk. Given that the devil had recently moved into her apartment, it kept spoiling on her.

* * *

By the time she returned home, Anna saw a dark figure in the driveway.

Hmm . . .

Demon or thief?

Human or ghoul?

She grabbed her Bio Freeze spray from under her seat—which was legal and more effective than pepper spray—as well as her holy water, just to cover all bases, and got out of her Jeep.

Making sure that she had her keys ready to open the front door, she headed for the stoop.

The shadow moved.

Anna lifted her arm to hose the shadow down with both bottles.

If one didn't work, the other would.

"Whoa there, Texarkana! Not the eyes!" The tall, gorgeous woman, clad in black leather, held her arm up to shield elaborate black makeup reminiscent of Brandon Lee in The Crow, except the lines were much more deliberate and defined, and appeared to be ancient alchemy symbols. "I'm not wearing waterproof mascara. Which in retrospect was a poor life decision, given my line of work."

Anna hesitated at the sight of this newcomer. Her straight, waist-length black hair was liberally streaked with gray, and pulled into a high ponytail. A solid black pentagram choker rested on her throat above a hematite pendulum that dangled between her ample breasts, which were barely covered by a loose fishnet top. The only thing that kept her transparent shirt from being obscene was a tight leather corset. She'd finished her bizarre outfit off with black crocheted shorts over skin-tight leather leggings and thigh high, stacked boots, along with a stylish leather coat that fell all the way to her ankles.

Yeah, they didn't dress this way back home. Anna had never quite seen anything like this woman in her life.

But the creepiest thing . . . her eyes were stark, crystal white in the darkness.

If those weren't theater contacts, that only left one conclusion . . .

"Are you one of my ghosts screwing with me?"

The woman snorted. "No."

"Then why are you dressed like an eighties social reject?"

"Ow!" She bristled indignantly. "Now that's a bit harsh, considering your father sent me here to watch over you, and help until his arrival."

Sucking her breath in sharply, Anna cringed with regret. Apparently, she'd been hanging out with her ex too much lately and had picked up his nastier personality traits. "I'm so sorry. I didn't mean to offend you. But you do look like you just stepped out of the movie, The Craft."

"First, that movie is from the nineties, and no, I don't. For your information, I was dressing like this long before the actors who starred in it were either born or house-broken. And for what I do, this outfit works well as it tends to scare away messy little kids, gross old men, and, best of all, it hides bloodstains." She flashed a mischievous grin. "Plus, it's easy to clean, and it's biodegradable."

Not what Anna was expecting the woman

to say by a long shot. And it definitely quelled any smart aleck retort she had. "Okay, then. I'm hoping you don't mean *my* blood."

"Me, too."

Well, that wasn't even a little comforting from where Anna was standing. "And for the record, you are?"

Crossing her arms over her chest, the woman sobered. "The Witch of Endor."

Anna arched a brow at another thing she wasn't expecting this stranger to say. "As in the biblical necromancer?"

Without a hint of humor, she inclined her head.

Anna was impressed, except for one thing she needed to straighten out. "I'm assuming by that, it's a title thing. You're not really the same woman who summoned up King Samuel. 'Cause that would make you what . . . a billion years old?"

She smirked. "Not quite. But yeah, I'm a bit long in the tooth."

Anna gaped at something that couldn't be real. Or true.

"Uzarah!"

Anna froze at the deep demonic growl that echoed from her building. "What was that?"

"The demon calling my name." She wrinkled her nose. "He and I are old friends. We basically cruised the Stone Age on dinosaurs together. Hung out. Brought down a few dynasties. Fun times."

Clearing her throat, she glanced toward Anna's apartment window without Anna having told her which one it was. "Achish, buddy! Are we really doing this?"

Lights exploded through the apartment building like a sped-up freaky Christmas exhibition on YouTube. A screeching howl started inside, then crescendoed louder and louder as it threatened to break windows and splinter Anna's eardrums.

Anna covered her ears and cringed in fear.

"Don't react to him. He's an attention hog. Like a pesky little brother. Ignore the brat and he'll stop."

To prove her point, Uzarah yawned.

The moment she did, the demon screamed and manifested in front of her in all his ugly, dark blue glory. Towering over the witch, he growled with flaming scarlet eyes.

Uzarah let out another exaggerated yawn and waved her hand over her mouth. Twice.

He gestured one clawed hand toward Anna. "I own her!"

Uzarah shrugged nonchalantly. "You

cheated. Like that's anything new, right? She didn't know she was giving up her soul. Do we really have to get lawyers involved?"

"She signed in blood!"

Arching a brow that somehow managed to question her sanity, Uzarah glanced over to Anna.

"No, I didn't!" Anna glared between them and stood on her tiptoes to drive home her point. "I know for a fact I didn't! I'd never do something *that* . . ." She froze as she remembered the pen she'd used in the realtor's office that had been sharp. It'd cut her finger an instant before she signed her papers. "Oh wait a second. They cut my hand on the pen and told me it was defective! That was extreme cheating!"

Horrified, Anna gaped at Uzarah. "Can they really count that? It was a trick."

With a tsk, the witch passed a sneer toward her old comrade. "Demons are crafty beasts. It's why they call it 'progressive entrapment.' They pretend to be your friends. Pretend to be helpful . . . then the minute you drop your guard, they bite you on your ass. Kind of like real friends, which is why I prefer not to have any . . . and family."

He laughed. "As I said, she's mine!"

Anna went cold as she saw the look of resignation on Uzarah's face.

"You're right, Achish. There's nothing I can do about it. But ..."

The demon tensed. "What?"

"I am a necromancer. I *can* release all the other souls you've claimed. Bring them back from the dead and have them come at you, bruh."

The demon's eyes flared. "You wouldn't dare!"

"Oh yes, I would. So, you have a choice. Her soul, or all the souls you've claimed? Which is it?"

The contract appeared instantly in his hand, then burst into flames. "She's free."

"And you will leave her alone while she moves out, and make sure all of your little buddies do the same, Achish. I mean it!"

"Fine!" He vanished.

Anna was aghast. "I can't believe it! How did you do that?" And so easily, too!

She shrugged. "A lot of centuries of negotiating. You just have to know who to call. How to hit low and with bonus points."

"Are there a lot of you?"

Uzarah shook her head. "Not anymore, thanks to Saul and a few others who didn't understand what we are, and why we were necessary to this world. And because of their rampant stupidity, I have to get back to my post before dawn. Give my best to your father. Tell him to finish our bargain so that your little realtor can't run her racket on innocent people here anymore."

"What do you mean? What racket?"

"She's the one who was really damned. And this was how she got out of her own contract. Treacherous bitch. To save her own soul, she replaced it with those of innocent people she brought in here. Your father has to close the portal she opened in the rooms so that she can't feed anymore lives to her demon. You need to make sure you're not around when that happens. Last thing you want is them yanking you through one to get back at your dad."

"You got it. Believe me, I've learned my lesson."

"And that is?"

"Be careful what you ask for. You just might get it. And whenever you sign a contract, *always* read the fine print. You never know when the lawyers are going to suck out your soul."

Also by

SHERRILYN KENYON

NEW TITLES

Eve of Destruction

Born of Blood

Dark Places

DARK-HUNTER®

Night Pleasures

Night Embrace

Dance with the Devil

Kiss of the Night

Night Play

Sword of Darkness

Knight of Darkness

Seize the Night

Sins of the Night

Unleash the Night

Dark Side of the Moon

Deadmen Walking
Death Doesn't Bargain
At Death's Door

Born of Night
Born of Fire
Born of Ice
Fire & Ice
Born of Shadows
Born of Silence
Cloak & Silence
Born of Fury
Born of Defiance
Born of Betrayal
Born of Legend
Born of Vengeance

Born of Blood
Born of Trouble
Born of Darkness

NICKCHRONICLES

Infinity

Invincible

Infamous

Inferno

Illusion

Instinct

Invision

Intensity

Lords of Avalon

(written as Kinley MacGregor)

Sword of Darkness

Knight of Darkness

About the Author

Defying all odds is what #1 New York Times and international bestselling author Sherrilyn Kenyon does best. Rising from extreme poverty as a child that culminated in being a homeless mother with an infant, she has become one of the most popular and influential authors in the world (in both adult and young adult fiction), with dedicated legions of fans known as Paladins–thousands of whom proudly sport tattoos from her numerous genre-defying series.

Since her first book debuted in 1993 while she was still in college, she has placed more than 80 novels on the New York Times list in all formats and genres, including manga and graphic novels, and has more than 70 million books in print worldwide. Her current series include: Dark-Hunters®, Chronicles of Nick®, Deadman's Cross™, Black Hat Society™, Nevermore™, Silent Swans™, Lords of Avalon® and The League®.

Over the years, her Lords of Avalon® novels have been adapted by Marvel, and her Dark-Hunters® and Chronicles of Nick® are New York Times bestselling manga and comics and are #1 bestselling adult coloring books.

Join her and her Paladins online at QueenofAllShadows.com and www.facebook.com/mysherrilyn.

Printed in the USA
CPSIA information can be obtained
at www.ICGtesting.com
LVHW092204280124
770188LV00022B/210/J